This book belongs to

This book is dedicated to my Son, my ray of light, my rainbow on rainy days, my super strength when I can't find my own, my little frappucino.

To my Nanny Ping, I'll see you again somewhere over a rainbow.

To all the Keyworkers, especially those on the front line; to my family, my friends near and far, and a special shout out to my sister, a keyworker, for giving me the support to continue with this; and of course to Shaun, my editor, without you this wouldn't have been possible.

To every single person who has helped with the production of this book and, of course, to all of the children who are being amazing and staying home. You are true superheroes.

To all the parents who are holding on each day: stay sane, you're doing wonderfully and especially to all the single mums and dads out there, who are doing the job of two parents - I feel you!

Once upon a time in a land we all once knew, lots of little boys and girls were staying at home...

The children didn't know why they were just enjoying having their parents to themselves. They got to cook and play all day - after a little school work, of course.

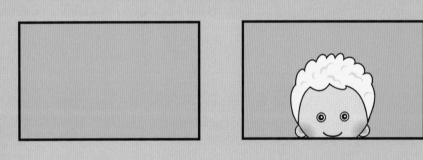

Outside their windows, while they were playing with their mummies and daddies, there were real superheroes that were about to save the world...

Captain Zoom
was super-speedy.

He could zoom through a city
in under a second. When people
needed a helping hand he was
there in a flash.

He was the best choice for the job as he could get there before anything even happened.

Agent Eye had night vision and could jump as high as the buildings.

He could see the whole city from the rooftops, where he kept watch for robbers and bad people, jumping down on them with a crash.

Night Star helped the elderly. She had super-strength and got her power from the moonlight.

Doctor Kind could capture the baddies and zap monsters through the air.

She fought them with science, magic potions and the need to end the evil in the world.

POW!

One day, Doctor Kind was tackling some naughty monsters when Captain Zoom came skidding into the room.

"Quick, Doctor, we need your help! The evil King of the Monster Kingdom has escaped and nobody can stop him!"

Dr. Kind peered out of the window and, sure enough, there was the King of the Monsters sucking the happiness out of everyone and crashing from building to building leaving not a person untouched.

"But I've used up all my strength fighting the little monsters all day", she said wearily.

"You're right. We surely can't do this alone," said Captain Zoom.

"Wait, what was it you were telling me about the children you've seen around the city," asked Dr. Kind.

CRASH

Captain Zoom had told her the previous evening that every night at 8pm people would cheer and clap at their doors and windows.

All of the children had also been painting rainbows with their parents and putting them in their windows for passers-by to see.

"I've got it!"
cried Dr. Kind delightedly.

"If we can mix the sound of the cheers with the rainbow light it will cause a great zing of energy and we can come together to charge our powers", she exclaimed.

ZING

SWOOSH

"Brilliant!" said Captain Zoom and rushed to tell the others the plan.

Night Star was out on the street. She'd already been protecting the elderly from the King.

Knowing they were weak he had attacked them, leaving many grandmas and grandads in fear.

Night Star had amazing strength. She moved cars and buses blocking the monsters path to slow him down.

She did this as she knew the old people would need time to get to a safe place.

Agent Eye was already on the rooftops looking for signs of help.

"One, two, three.... four... just a few more, it's working. We'll soon be able to charge our powers," he said hopefully.

Captain Zoom arrived on the rooftop. Within half an hour the streets began to glisten with multi-colours.

SWOOSH

Captain Zoom grabbed his cloak and zipped into the air.

He had to make it faster than ever this time so he swooped down to Night Star, grabbing her just before the naughty King came crashing down on her.

"You took your time," laughed Night Star.

They flew away as the king took a huge gasp of air and sent a hurricane chasing right after them.

But Captain Zoom was quicker. He made it to Dr. Kind, took her by the hand and shouted "Let's go!"

They arrived on the rooftop just in time: the cheers had become louder and the whole sky was full of colour.

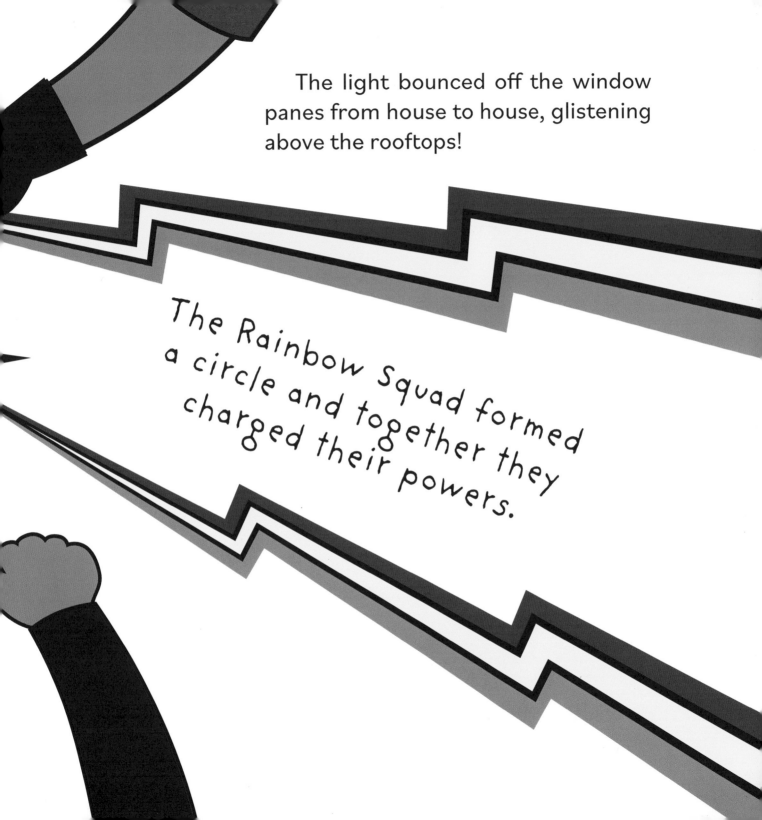

The light bounced off the window panes from house to house, glistening above the rooftops!

The Rainbow Squad formed a circle and together they charged their powers.

Soon all of the people returned to their houses, and the streets were still and quiet.

"Do you think it was enough?" asked Agent Eye. "I can see the King from here, he's travelled quite far since we were gone."

"There's only one way to find out," said Night Star. "Let's Go!"

They jumped from high, down to the street towards the evil King.

He roared as they came close, sending a big gust of air towards them and knocking them off their feet.

Agent Eye grabbed his baton from his side and threw it furiously towards the King, just missing him.

CRASH

But Agent Eye had seen what was about to happen and jumped above him to send it crashing right through his crown.

He had been weakened, but he wasn't giving up yet...

Night Star produced a wisp of enchanted moonlight and ran directly at the monster tying it around his feet.

Captain Zoom pulled it with all the strength he could and the mean King came crashing to the ground, turning off all the lights in the city as he fell. But he still hadn't been defeated.

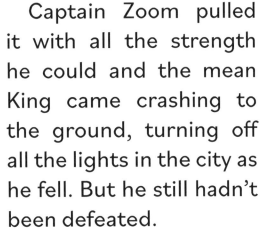

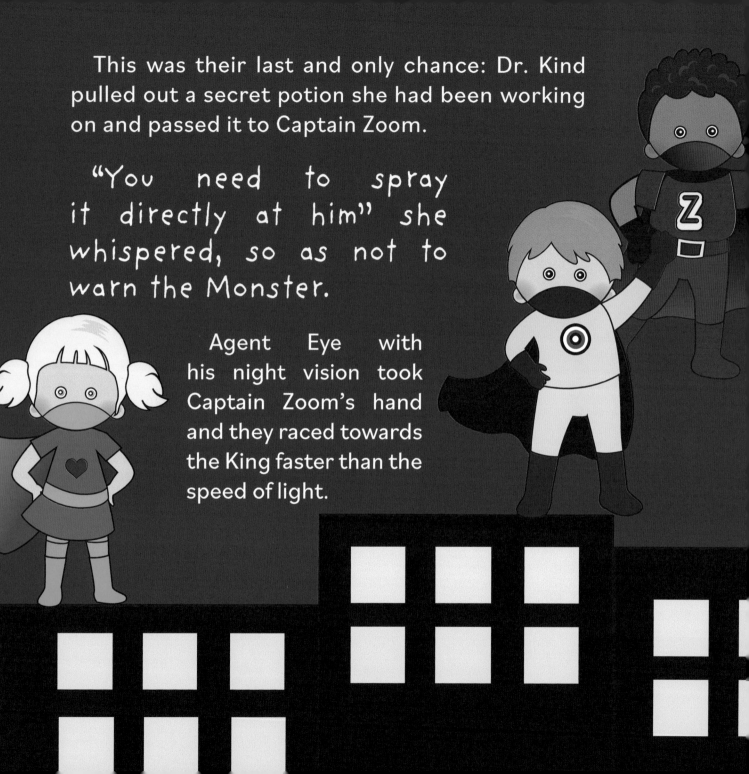

This was their last and only chance: Dr. Kind pulled out a secret potion she had been working on and passed it to Captain Zoom.

"You need to spray it directly at him" she whispered, so as not to warn the Monster.

Agent Eye with his night vision took Captain Zoom's hand and they raced towards the King faster than the speed of light.

Splat! Boom! Bang! went the potion. The shocked King let out a huge groan and, in a puff of smoke, he was gone!

They had done it!
They had won.

Together, with their different abilities they
had finally made the evil King disappear.

The next morning everything was back to normal. The little children were amazed at the stories of how the naughty monster had finally been destroyed.

They sang, they played with their friends in the parks and there was also talk of them finally going back to school.

The Rainbow Squad were so happy for all the help from the little children that they wanted to say a huge thank you!

At 8pm that night, Captain Zoom sent letters to each and every child.

He filled the streets with balloons and everywhere was full of happiness as the children danced in the colourful streets with their families and friends.

They all went to bed full of excitement, knowing that with their help the King had gone forever.

They were the real superheroes looking towards a very bright and colourful future.

Printed in Great Britain
by Amazon

22116592R00018